Library of Congress Cataloging-in-Publication Data is available.
ISBN 978-0-06-124405-6 (trade bdg.)
ISBN 978-0-06-124406-3 (lib. bdg.)

Typography by Stephanie Bart-Horvath
6 7 8 9 10
❖
First Edition

To Samantha
~E.K.

To Maria
~V.K.

Purplicious

Written by
Victoria Kann &
Elizabeth Kann

Illustrated by
Victoria Kann

HarperCollinsPublishers

I was in art class, painting a picture.

"What are you painting?" asked Kendra.
"A picture of a sunset," I said.
"Eww, it's sooooo ugly. Pinkalicious, why does everything you paint have to have pink in it?" asked Tara.

"Because pink is my favorite color,"
I answered.

"Don't you know, pink is *passé*. *Passé* is
French for 'over,'" said Brittany. "The new
color is black. *All* the girls like black now."

"Black is in," said Beatrice during recess.
"Pink is putrid," announced Pauline while
dangling from the monkey bars.
"Yeah, pink stinks!" added Sophia.

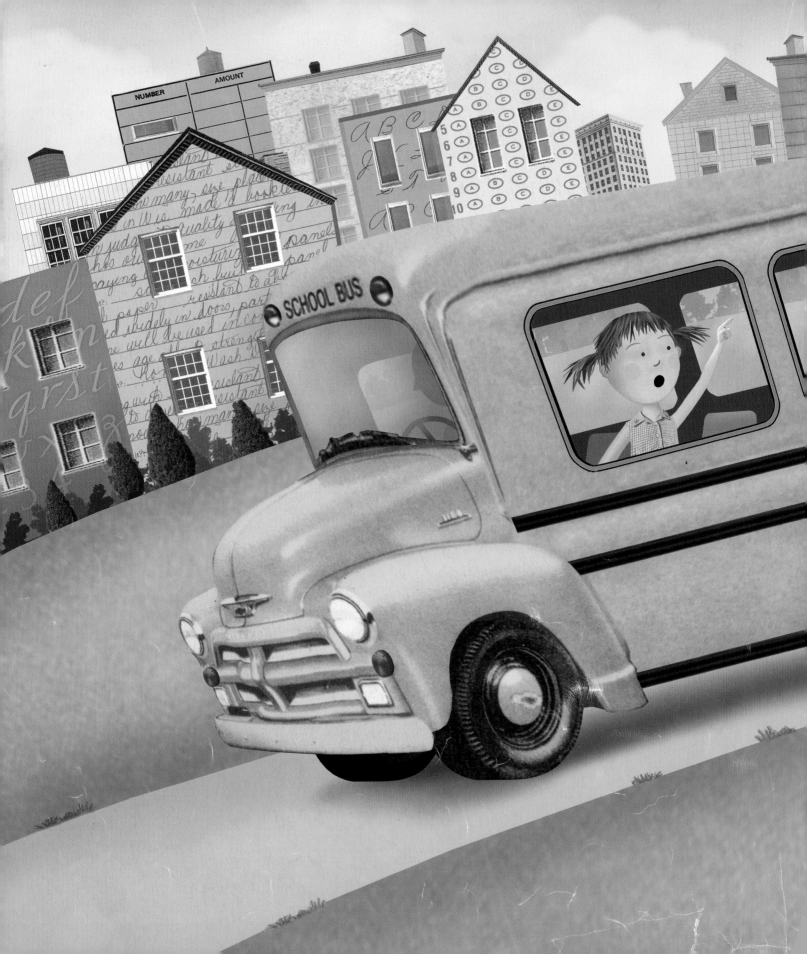

On the bus ride home from school, no one would sit with me.

"Pink is for babies and little girls. We aren't going to be friends with a baaaby," taunted Tiffany.

"You don't have to be a baby or a little girl to like the color pink. Pink is for everyone," I said. "Even my brother likes pink."

"How funny! A boy who likes pink?!" Everyone on the bus laughed. "Isn't it time you moved *beyond* pink?"

After school no one would play princess with me.
I went to my room and counted all my pink things.
I had a pink phone, a pink crayon, a pink piggy bank,
pink underwear, a pink tiara, even a giant pink
bunny. I had more than a hundred pink possessions.
The only black thing I had was an ugly plastic spider
left over from Halloween.

I wrote with my pink pen in my pink diary:

That week, after the girls teased me
in school, I wrote in my diary every day.
Then I cried into my pink hankie.

<u>Wednesday</u>
Pink makes
me happy
but mean
girls make
me sad.

<u>Friday</u>
pink
has no
purpose.

<u>Thursday</u>
pink is
a lonely
color.

On Saturday, Mommy, Daddy, Peter, and I
went to get ice cream to cheer me up.

"Pinkalicious, what would you like?" asked Mr. Swizzle. "Magenta Mint Mango, or perhaps you would enjoy Pink Passion Fruit Paradise? Today's special flavor is Pleasing Pomegranate Punch."

"No thanks. I'll just have . . . um . . . vanilla." I sighed, looking around to see who might see me from my school.

"How about you, Peter? Would you like your usual, Plum Pink Perfection?"

"Yes! Yes, thank you!" said Peter.
"You're such a baby, Peter. Pink ice
cream is for sissies!" I said.

"Pinkalicious, aren't you going to
eat your ice cream?" asked Mommy.
"Well, I'm actually not that hungry."
The ice cream tasted bland to me.
I couldn't possibly eat it.

"Pinkalicious has the blues," Daddy said that night
when I wouldn't play pink-pong with him.

"What does it mean when you have the blues?" I asked.

"It means that you feel sad. Why do you feel sad?"

"No one will play with me because I like the color pink.
All the girls like the color black now and I don't."

"Are you sure *all* the girls like black? Maybe there are
other kids who like pink."

"Everyone hates pink. You don't know anything!"
I screamed, running to my room.

"I'm the only one in the whole wide world who likes pink. I am all alone. No one understands me," I said to myself.

On Monday I noticed a girl in art class.
She was painting a beautiful picture.
"What are you painting?" I asked.
"It's a picture of a cake, but the blue
frosting doesn't look right. I think I need
some pink, and then it will be perfect."

"Really?" I asked. "You *like* pink?
Don't you think pink is for babies?"
"Pink is perfect," she answered.
"Watch this and you'll see why. . . ."

She mixed the pink paint into the blue, and the frosting turned purple.
"Pink is powerful," she said. "Look, it turned blue into purple."
"Hmmm, purple is pretty," I said.

"Not just pretty . . . it's purplicious!"